Dear Mr. Henshaw

YEARLING BOOKS/YOUNG YEARLINGS/YEARLING CLASSICS are designed especially to entertain and enlighten young people. Patricia Reilly Giff, consultant to this series, received her bachelor's degree from Marymount College and a master's degree in history from St. John's University. She holds a Professional Diploma in Reading and a Doctorate of Humane Letters from Hofstra University. She was a teacher and reading consultant for many years, and is the author of numerous books for young readers.

BEVERLY CLEARY

Dear Mr. Henshaw

ILLUSTRATED BY PAUL O. ZELINSKY

A YEARLING BOOK

Published by
Dell Publishing
a division of
Bantam Doubleday Dell Publishing Group, Inc.
1540 Broadway
New York, New York 10036

ISBN: 0-440-21934-5

Reprinted by arrangement with
William Morrow and Company, Inc.

Printed in the United States of America

August 1984

10 9 8 7 6 5 4 3

RAD

Dear Mr. Henshaw

Dear Mr. Henshaw,

My teacher read your book about the dog to our class. It was funny. We licked it.

Your freind,

Leigh Botts (boy)

Dear Mr. Henshaw,

I am the boy who wrote to you last year when I was in the second grade. Maybe you didn't get my letter. This year I read the book I wrote to you about called *Ways to Amuse a Dog.* It is the first thick book with chapters that I have read.

The boy's father said city dogs were bored so Joe could not keep the dog unless he could think up seven ways to amuse it. I have a black dog. His name is Bandit. He is a nice dog.

If you answer I get to put your letter on the bulletin board.

My teacher taught me a trick about friend. The *i* goes before *e* so that at the end it will spell *end*.

Keep in tutch.

> Your fri*end*,
> Leigh (Lēē) Botts

Dear Mr. Henshaw,

I am in the fourth grade now. I made a diorama of *Ways to Amuse a Dog*, the book I wrote to you about two times before. Now our teacher is making us write to authors for Book Week. I got your answer to my letter last year, but it was only printed. Please would you write to me in your own handwriting? I am a great enjoyer of your books.

My favorite character in the book was Joe's Dad because he didn't get mad when Joe amused his dog by playing a tape of a lady singing, and his dog sat and howled like he was singing, too. Bandit does the same thing when he hears singing.

Your best reader,
Leigh Botts

December 2

Dear Mr. Henshaw,

I got to thinking about *Ways to Amuse a Dog*. When Joe took his dog to the park and taught him to slide down the slide, wouldn't some grownup come along and say he couldn't let his dog use the slide? Around here grownups, who are mostly real old with cats, get mad if dogs aren't on leashes every minute. I hate living in a mobile home park.

I saw your picture on the back of the book. When I grow up I want to be a famous book writer with a beard like you.

I am sending you my picture. It is last year's picture. My hair is longer now. With all the millions of kids in the U.S., how would you know who I am if I don't send you my picture?

                          Your favorite reader,
                          Leigh Botts

Enclosure: Picture of me.
(We are studying
business letters.)

October 2

Dear Mr. Henshaw,

I am in the fifth grade now. You might like to know that I gave a book report on *Ways to Amuse a Dog*. The class liked it. I got an A–. The minus was because the teacher said I didn't stand on both feet.

Sincerely,
Leigh Botts

Dear Mr. Henshaw,

I got your letter and did what you said. I read a different book by you. I read *Moose on Toast*. I liked it almost as much as *Ways to Amuse a Dog*. It was really funny the way the boy's mother tried to think up ways to cook the moose meat they had in their freezer. 1000 pounds is a lot of moose. Mooseburgers, moose stew and moose meat loaf don't sound too bad. Maybe moose mincemeat pie would be OK because with all the raisins and junk you wouldn't know you were eating moose. Creamed chipped moose on toast, yuck.

I don't think the boy's father should have shot the moose, but I guess there are plenty of moose up there in Alaska, and maybe they needed it for food.

If my Dad shot a moose I would feed the tough parts to my dog Bandit.

Your number 1 fan,
Leigh Botts

September 20

Dear Mr. Henshaw,

This year I am in the sixth grade in a new school in a different town. Our teacher is making us do author reports to improve our writing skills, so of course I thought of you. Please answer the following questions.

1. How many books have you written?
2. Is Boyd Henshaw your real name or is it fake?
3. Why do you write books for children?
4. Where do you get your ideas?
5. Do you have any kids?
6. What is your favorite book that you wrote?
7. Do you like to write books?
8. What is the title of your next book?
9. What is your favorite animal?
10. Please give me some tips on how to write a book. This is important to me. I really want to know so I can get to be a famous author and write books exactly like yours.

Please send me a list of your books that you wrote, an autographed picture and a bookmark. I need your answer by next Friday. This is urgent!

Sincerely,
Leigh Botts

De Liver
De Letter
De Sooner
De Better
De Later
De Letter
De Madder
I Getter

Dear Mr. Henshaw,

At first I was pretty upset when I didn't get an answer to my letter in time for my report, but I worked it out OK. I read what it said about you on the back of *Ways to Amuse a Dog* and wrote real big on every other line so I filled up the paper. On the book it said you lived in Seattle, so I didn't know you had moved to Alaska although I should have guessed from *Moose on Toast.*

When your letter finally came I didn't want to read it to the class, because I didn't think Miss Martinez would like silly answers, like your real name is Messing A. Round, and you don't have kids because you don't raise goats. She said I had to read it. The class laughed and Miss Martinez smiled, but she didn't smile when I came to the part about your favorite animal was a purple monster who ate children who sent authors long lists of questions for reports instead of learning to use the library.

Your writing tips were OK. I could tell you meant what you said. Don't worry. When I write something, I won't send it to you. I understand how busy you are with your own books.

I hid the second page of your letter from Miss Martinez. That list of questions you sent for me to answer really made me mad. Nobody else's author put in a list of questions to be answered, and I don't think it's fair to make me do more work when I already wrote a report.

Anyway, thank you for answering my questions. Some kids didn't get any answers at all, which made them mad, and one girl almost cried, she was so afraid she would get a bad grade. One boy got a letter from an author who sounded real excited about getting a letter and wrote such a long answer the boy had to write a long report. He guessed nobody ever wrote to that author before, and he sure wouldn't again. About ten kids wrote to the same author, who wrote one answer to all of them. There was a big argument about who got to keep it until Miss Martinez took the letter to the office and duplicated it.

About those questions you sent me. I'm not going to answer them, and you can't make me. You're not my teacher.

Yours truly,

Leigh Botts

P.S. When I asked you what the title of your next book was going to be, you said, Who knows? Did you mean that was the title or you don't know what the title will be? And do you really write books because you have read every book in the library and because writing beats mowing the lawn or shoveling snow?

Dear Mr. Henshaw,

Mom found your letter and your list of questions which I was dumb enough to leave lying around. We had a big argument. She says I have to answer your questions because authors are working people like anyone else, and if you took time to answer my questions, I should answer yours. She says I can't go through life expecting everyone to do everything for me. She used to say the same thing to Dad when he left his socks on the floor.

Well, I got to go now. It's bedtime. Maybe I'll get around to answering your ten questions, and maybe I won't. There isn't any law that says I have to. Maybe I won't even read any more of your books.

Disgusted reader,
Leigh Botts

P.S. If my Dad was here, he would tell you to go climb a tree.

Dear Mr. Henshaw,

Mom is nagging me about your dumb old questions. She says if I really want to be an author, I should follow the tips in your letter. I should read, look, listen, think and <u>write</u>. She says the best way she knows for me to get started is to apply the seat of my pants to a chair and answer your questions and answer them fully. So here goes.

1. Who are you?

Like I've been telling you, I am Leigh Botts. Leigh Marcus Botts. I don't like Leigh for a name because some people don't know how to say it or think it's a girl's name. Mom says with a last name like Botts I need something fancy but not too fancy. My Dad's name is Bill and Mom's name is Bonnie. She says Bill and Bonnie Botts sounds like something out of a comic strip.

I am just a plain boy. This school doesn't say

I am Gifted and Talented, and I don't like soccer very much the way everybody at this school is supposed to. I am not stupid either.

2. *What do you look like?*

I already sent you my picture, but maybe you lost it. I am sort of medium. I don't have red hair or anything like that. I'm not real big like my Dad. Mom says I take after her family, thank goodness. That's the way she always says it. In first and second grades kids used to call me Leigh the Flea, but I have grown. Now when the class lines up according to height, I am in the middle. I guess you could call me the mediumest boy in the class.

This is hard work. To be continued, maybe.

Leigh Botts

Dear Mr. Henshaw,

I wasn't going to answer any more of your questions, but Mom won't get the TV repaired because she says it was rotting my brain. This is Thanksgiving vacation and I am so bored I decided to answer a couple of your rotten questions with my rotten brain. (Joke.)

3. *What is your family like?*

Since Dad and Bandit went away, my family is just Mom and me. We all used to live in a mobile home outside of Bakersfield which is in California's Great Central Valley we studied about in school. When Mom and Dad got divorced, they sold the mobile home, and Dad moved into a trailer.

Dad drives a big truck, a cab-over job. That means the cab is over the engine. Some people don't know that. The truck is why my parents got divorced. Dad used to drive for someone else, hauling stuff like cotton, sugar beets and other produce around Central California and Nevada, but he couldn't get owning his own rig for cross-country hauling out of his head. He worked practically night and day and saved a down payment. Mom said we'd never get out of that mobile home when he had to make such big payments on that rig, and she'd never know where he was when he hauled cross-country. His big rig sure is a beauty, with a bunk in the cab and everything. His rig, which truckers call a tractor but everyone else calls a truck, has ten wheels, two in front and eight in back so he can hitch up to anything—flatbeds, refrigerated vans, a couple of gondolas.

In school they teach you that a gondola is some kind of boat in Italy, but in the U.S. it is a container for hauling loose stuff like carrots.

My hand is all worn out from all this writing, but I try to treat Mom and Dad the same so I'll get to Mom next time.

Your pooped reader,
Leigh Botts

November 23

Mr. Henshaw:

Why should I call you "dear," when you are the reason I'm stuck with all this work? It wouldn't be fair to leave Mom out so here is Question 3 continued.

Mom works part time for Catering by Katy which is run by a real nice lady Mom knew when she was growing up in Taft, California. Katy says all women who grew up in Taft had to be good cooks because they went to so many potluck suppers. Mom and Katy and some other ladies make fancy food for weddings and parties. They also bake cheesecake and apple strudel for restaurants. Mom is a good cook. I just wish she would do it more at home, like the mother in *Moose on Toast*. Almost every day Katy gives Mom something good to put in my school lunch.

Mom also takes a couple of courses at the community college. She wants to be an LVN which means Licensed Vocational Nurse.

They help real nurses except they don't stick needles in people. She is almost always home when I get home from school.

Your ex-friend,
Leigh Botts

Mr. Henshaw:

Here we go again.

4. *Where do you live?*

After the divorce Mom and I moved from Bakersfield to Pacific Grove which is on California's Central Coast about twenty miles from the sugar refinery at Spreckels where Dad used to haul sugar beets before he went cross-country. Mom said all the time she was growing

up in California's Great Central Valley she longed for a few ocean breezes, and now we've got them. We've got a lot of fog, especially in the morning. There aren't any crops around here, just golf courses for rich people.

We live in a little house, a *really* little house, that used to be somebody's summer cottage a long time ago before somebody built a two-story duplex in front of it. Now it is what they call a garden cottage. It is sort of falling apart, but it is all we can afford. Mom says at least it keeps the rain off, and it can't be hauled away on a flatbed truck. I have a room of my own, but Mom sleeps on a couch in the living room. She fixed the place up real nice with things from the thrift shop down the street.

Next door is a gas station that goes ping-ping, ping-ping every time a car drives in. They turn off the pinger at 10:00 P.M., but most of the time I am asleep by then. Mom doesn't want me to hang around the gas station. On our street, besides the thrift shop, there is a pet shop, a sewing machine shop, an electric shop, a couple of junk stores they call antique shops, plus a Taco King and a Softee Freeze. I am not supposed to hang around those places either. Mom is against hanging around anyplace.

Sometimes when the gas station isn't ping-ing, I can hear the ocean and the sea lions bark-ing. They sound like dogs, and I think of Bandit.

To be continued unless we get the TV fixed.

Still disgusted,

Leigh Botts

Mr. Henshaw:

If our TV was fixed I would be looking at "Highway Patrol," but it isn't so here are some more answers from my rotten brain. (Ha-ha.)

5. *Do you have any pets?*

I do not have any pets. (My teacher says always answer questions in complete sentences.) When Mom and Dad got divorced and Mom got me, Dad took Bandit because Mom said she couldn't work and look after a dog, and Dad said he likes to take Bandit in his truck because it is easier to stay awake on long hauls if he has him to talk to. I really miss Bandit, but I guess he's happier riding around with Dad. Like the father said in *Ways to Amuse a Dog*, dogs get pretty bored just lying around the house all day. That is what Bandit would have to do with Mom and me gone so much.

Bandit likes to ride. That's how we got him. He just jumped into Dad's cab at a truck stop in Nevada and sat there. He had a red bandanna around his neck instead of a collar, so we called him Bandit.

Sometimes I lie awake at night listening to the gas station ping-pinging and thinking about Dad and Bandit hauling tomatoes or cotton bales on Interstate 5, and I am glad Bandit is there to keep Dad awake. Have you ever seen Interstate 5? It is straight and boring with nothing much but cotton fields and a big feedlot that you can smell a long way before you come to it. It is so boring that the cattle on the feedlot don't even bother to moo. They just stand there. They don't tell you that part in school when they talk about California's Great Central Valley.

I'm getting writer's cramp from all this writing. I'll get to No. 6 next time. Mom says not to worry about the postage, so I can't use that as an excuse for not answering.

Pooped writer,
Leigh Botts

Mr. Henshaw:

Here we go again. I'll never write another list of questions for an author to answer, no matter what the teacher says.

6. *Do you like school?*

School is OK, I guess. That's where the kids are. The best thing about sixth grade in my new school is that if I hang in, I'll get out.

7. *Who are your friends?*

I don't have a whole lot of friends in my new school. Mom says maybe I'm a loner, but I don't know. A new boy in school has to be pretty cautious until he gets to know who's who. Maybe I'm just a boy nobody pays much attention to. The only time anybody paid much attention to me was in my last school when I gave the book report on *Ways to Amuse a Dog*. After my report some people went to the library to get the book. The kids here pay more attention to my lunch than they do to me. They really watch to see what I have in my lunch because Katy gives me such good things.

I wish somebody would ask me over sometime. After school I stay around kicking a soccer ball with some of the other kids so they won't think I am stuck up or anything, but nobody asks me over.

8. Who is your favorite teacher?

I don't have a favorite teacher, but I really like Mr. Fridley. He's the custodian. He's always fair about who gets to pass out milk at lunchtime, and once when he had to clean up after someone who threw up in the hall, he didn't even look cross. He just said, "Looks like somebody's been whooping it up," and started sprinkling sawdust around. Mom used to get mad at Dad for whooping it up, but she didn't mean throwing up. She meant he stayed too long at that truck stop outside of town.

Two more questions to go. Maybe I won't answer them. So there. Ha-ha.

Leigh Botts

Mr. Henshaw:

OK, you win, because Mom is still nagging me, and I don't have anything else to do. I'll answer your last two questions if it takes all night.

9. What bothers you?

What bothers me about what? I don't know what you mean. I guess I'm bothered by a lot of things. I am bothered when someone steals something out of my lunchbag. I don't know enough about the people in the school to know who to suspect. I am bothered about little kids with runny noses. I don't mean I am fussy or anything like that. I don't know why. I am just bothered.

I am bothered about walking to school *slow*. The rule is nobody is supposed to be on the school grounds until ten minutes before the first bell rings. Mom has an early class. The house is so lonely in the morning when she is gone that I can't stand it and leave when she does. I don't mind being alone after school, but I do in the morning before the fog lifts and our cottage seems dark and damp.

Mom tells me to go to school but to walk slow which is hard work. Once I tried walking around every square in the sidewalk, but that got boring. So did walking heel-toe, heel-toe. Sometimes I walk backwards except when I cross the street, but I still get there so early I have to sort of hide behind the shrubbery so Mr. Fridley won't see me.

I am bothered when my Dad telephones me and finishes by saying, "Well, keep your nose clean, kid." Why can't he say he misses me, and why can't he call me Leigh? I am bothered when he doesn't phone at all which is most of the time. I have a book of road maps and try to follow his trips when I hear from him. When the TV worked I watched the weather on the news so I would know if he was driving through blizzards, tornadoes, hail like golf balls or any of that fancy weather they have other places in the U.S.

10. What do you wish?

I wish somebody would stop stealing the good stuff out of my lunchbag. I guess I wish a lot of other things, too. I wish someday Dad and Bandit would pull up in front in the rig. Maybe Dad would be hauling a forty-foot reefer (that means refrigerated trailer) which would make his outfit add up to eighteen wheels altogether. Dad would yell out of the cab, "Come on, Leigh. Hop in and I'll give you a lift to school." Then I'd climb in and Bandit would wag his tail and lick my face. We'd take off with all the men in the gas station staring after us. Instead of going straight to school, we'd go barreling along the freeway looking down on the tops of ordinary cars, then down the offramp and back to school just before the bell rang. I guess I wouldn't seem so medium then, sitting up there in the cab in front of a forty-foot reefer. I'd jump out, and Dad would say, "So long, Leigh. Be seeing you," and Bandit would give a little bark like good-bye. I'd say, "Drive carefully, Dad," like I always do.

Dad would take a minute to write in the truck's logbook, "Drove my son to school." Then the truck would pull away from the curb with all the kids staring and wishing their Dads drove big trucks, too.

There, Mr. Henshaw. That's the end of your crummy questions. I hope you are satisfied for making me do all this extra work.

Fooey on you,
Leigh Botts

Dear Mr. Henshaw,

I am sorry I was rude in my last letter when I finished answering your questions. Maybe I was mad about other things, like Dad forgetting to send this month's support payment. Mom tried to phone him at the trailer park where, as Mom says, he hangs his hat. He has his own phone in his trailer so the broker who lines up jobs for him can reach him. I wish he still hauled sugar beets over to the refinery in Spreckels so he might come to see me. The judge in the divorce said he has a right to see me.

When you answered my questions, you said the way to get to be an author was to <u>write</u>. You underlined it twice. Well, I sure did a lot of writing, and you know what? Now that I think about it, it wasn't so bad when it wasn't for a book report or a report on some country in South America or anything where I had to look things up in the library. I even sort of miss

31

writing now that I've finished your questions. I get lonesome. Mom is working overtime at Catering by Katy because people give a lot of parties this time of year.

When I write a book maybe I'll call it *The Great Lunchbag Mystery*, because I have a lot of trouble with my lunchbag. Mom isn't so great on cooking roasts and steaks now that Dad is gone, but she makes me good lunches with sandwiches on whole wheat bread from the health food store with good filling spread all the way to the corners. Katy sends me little cheese-cakes baked just for me or stuffed mushrooms and little things she calls canapés (kà-nà-pāýs). Sometimes I get a slice of quiche (kēēsh).

Today I was supposed to have a deviled egg. Katy buys the smallest eggs for parties so half an egg can be eaten in one bite and won't spill on people's carpets. She puts a little curry pow-der in with the mashed-up yolk which she squirts out of a tube so it looks like a rose. At lunchtime when I opened my lunchbag, my

egg was gone. We leave our lunchbags and boxes (mostly bags because no sixth grader wants to carry a lunchbox) lined up along the wall under our coathooks at the back of the classroom behind a sort of partition.

Are you writing another book? Please answer my letter so we can be pen pals.

Still your No. 1 fan,
Leigh Botts

Dear Mr. Henshaw,

I was surprised to get your postcard from Wyoming, because I thought you lived in Alaska.

Don't worry. I get the message. You don't have a lot of time for answering letters. That's OK with me, because I'm glad you are busy writing a book and chopping wood to keep warm.

Something nice happened today. When I was hanging around behind the bushes at school waiting for the ten minutes to come before the first bell rings, I was watching Mr. Fridley raise the flags. Maybe I better explain that the state flag of California is white with a brown bear in the middle. First Mr. Fridley fastened the U.S. flag on the halyard (that's a new word in my vocabulary) and then fastened the California flag below it. When he pulled the flags to the top of the flagpole, the bear was upside down with his feet in the air. I said,

"Hey, Mr. Fridley, the bear is upside down."

This is a new paragraph because Miss Martinez says there should be a new paragraph when a different person speaks. Mr. Fridley said, "Well, so it is. How would you like to turn him right side up?"

So I got to pull the flags down, turn the bear flag the right way and raise both flags again. Mr. Fridley said maybe I should come to school a few minutes early every morning to help him with the flags, but please stop walking backwards because it made him nervous. So now I don't have to walk quite so slow. It was nice to have somebody notice me. Nobody stole anything from my lunch today because I ate it on the way to school.

I've been thinking about what you said on your postcard about keeping a diary. Maybe I'll try it.

Sincerely,
Leigh Botts

Dear Mr. Henshaw,

I bought a composition book like you said. It is yellow with a spiral binding. On the front I printed

DIARY OF LEIGH MARCUS BOTTS
PRIVATE—KEEP OUT
THIS MEANS YOU!!!!!

When I started to write in it, I didn't know how to begin. I felt as if I should write, "Dear Composition Book," but that sounds dumb. So does "Dear Piece of Paper." The first page still looks the way I feel. Blank. I don't think I can keep a diary. I don't want to be a nuisance to you, but I wish you could tell me how. I am stuck.

Puzzled reader,
Leigh Botts

Dear Mr. Henshaw,

I got your postcard with the picture of the bears. Maybe I'll do what you said and pretend my diary is a letter to somebody. I suppose I could pretend to write to Dad, but I used to write to him and he never answered. Maybe I'll pretend I am writing to you because when I answered all your questions, I got the habit of beginning, "Dear Mr. Henshaw." Don't worry. I won't send it to you.

Thanks for the tip. I know you're busy.

Your grateful friend,
Leigh Botts

PRIVATE DIARY OF LEIGH BOTTS

Friday, December 22

Dear Mr. Pretend Henshaw,

This is a diary. I will keep it, not mail it.

If I eat my lunch on the way to school, I get hungry in the afternoon. Today I didn't so the two stuffed mushrooms Mom packed in my lunch were gone at lunch period. My sandwich was still there so I didn't starve to death, but I sure missed those mushrooms. I can't complain to the teacher because it isn't a good idea for a new boy in school to be a snitch.

All morning I try to keep track of who leaves his seat to go behind the partition where we keep our lunches, and I watch to see who leaves the room last at recess. I haven't caught anybody chewing, but Miss Martinez is always telling me to face the front of the room. Anyway, the classroom door is usually open. Anybody could sneak in if we were all facing front and Miss Martinez was writing on the blackboard.

Hey, I just had an idea! Some authors write under made-up names. After Christmas vacation I'll write a fictitious name on my lunchbag. That will foil the thief, as they say in books.

I guess I don't have to sign my name to a diary letter the way I sign a real letter that I would mail.

Saturday, December 23

Dear Mr. Pretend Henshaw,

This is the first day of Christmas vacation. Still no package from Dad. I thought maybe he was bringing me a present instead of mailing it, so I asked Mom if she thought he might come to see us for Christmas.

She said, "We're divorced. Remember?"

I remember all right. I remember all the time.

Dear Mr. Pretend Henshaw,

Still no package from Dad.

I keep thinking about last Christmas when we were in the mobile home before Dad bought the tractor. He had to dodge the highway patrol to get home in time for Christmas. Mom cooked a turkey and a nice dinner. We had a Christmas tree about two feet high because there wasn't room for a big one.

At dinner Dad remarked that when he was driving along, he often saw one shoe lying on the highway. He always wondered how it got there and what happened to its mate.

Mom said one shoe sounded sad, like a country-western song. While we ate our mince pie we all tried to think up songs about lost shoes. I'll never forget them. Mine was worst:

> Driving with a heavy load
> I saw a shoe upon the road
> Squashed like a toad.

Dad came up with:

> I saw a shoe
> Wet with dew
> On Highway 2.
> It made me blue.
> What'll I do?

Mom's song really made us laugh. It was the best.

> A lonesome hiker was unluckee
> To lose his boot near Truckee.
> He hitched a ride with one foot damp
> Down the road to Angels Camp.

Dumb songs, but we had a lot of fun. Mom and Dad hadn't laughed that much for a long time, and I hoped they would never stop.

After that, whenever Dad came home, I asked if he had seen any shoes on the highway. He always had.

Dear Mr. Pretend Henshaw,

Last night I was feeling low and was still awake after the gas station stopped pinging. Then I heard heavy feet coming up the steps, and for a minute I thought it was Dad until I remembered he always ran up steps.

Mom is careful about opening the door at night. I heard her turn on the outside light and knew she was peeking out from behind the curtain. She opened the door, and a man said, "Is this where Leigh Botts lives?"

I was out of bed and into the front room in a second. "I'm Leigh Botts," I said.

"Your Dad asked me to drop this off for you." A man who looked like a trucker handed me a big package.

"Thanks," I said. "Thanks a whole lot." I must have looked puzzled because he said, "He sent out a call over his CB radio for someone coming to Pacific Grove who would like to play Santa. So here I am. Merry Christmas and a ho-ho-ho!" He waved and was off down the walk before I could say anything more.

"Wow!" I said to Mom. "Wow!" She just stood there in her robe smiling while I began to tear off the paper even if it wasn't Christmas morning. Dad had sent what I always wanted —a quilted down jacket with a lot of pockets and a hood that zips into the collar. I tried it on over my pajamas. It was the right size and felt great. Getting a present from my Dad in time for Christmas felt even better.

Today Katy invited us for Christmas dinner even though this has been a busy season for catering. She also had some of the other women who work with her and their kids and a few old people from her neighborhood.

On the way home Mom said, "Katy has a heart as big as a football stadium. It was a lovely dinner for lonely hearts."

I wondered if she was thinking about last Christmas when we tried to make up songs about lonely lost shoes.

Wednesday, January 3

Dear Mr. Pretend Henshaw,

I got behind in my diary during Christmas vacation because I had a lot of things to do such as go to the dentist for a checkup, get some new shoes and do a lot of things that don't get done during school.

Today I wrote a fictitious name, or pseud. as they sometimes say, on my lunchbag. I printed Joe Kelly on it because that was the name of the boy in *Ways to Amuse a Dog* so I knew it was fictitious. I guess I fooled the thief because nobody stole the water chestnuts and chicken livers wrapped in bacon that Katy broiled just for me. They are good even when they are cold. I hope the thief drooled when he watched me eat them.

Monday, January 8

Dear Mr. Pretend Henshaw,

Dad phoned me from Hermiston, Oregon! I just looked in my book of road maps and saw where it is, up there by the Columbia River. He said he was waiting for a load of potatoes. I could hear a juke box and a bunch of men talking. I asked about Bandit, and he said Bandit was fine, a great listener on a long haul even though he doesn't have much to say. I asked Dad if I could ride with him sometime next summer when school is out, and he said he'd see. (I *hate* answers like that.) Anyway, he said he was sending the support check and he was sorry he forgot and he hoped I liked the jacket.

I sure wish Dad lived with us again, but he said he would phone in about a week and to keep my nose clean. He had to go to make sure the potatoes were loaded so they wouldn't shift going around curves.

This has been a good day. My lunch was safe again.

Mr. Fridley is so funny. Lots of kids are having their teeth straightened so when they eat lunch, they take out their retainers and wrap them in paper napkins while they eat because nobody wants to look at a spitty retainer. Sometimes they forget and throw the napkin with the retainer into the garbage. Then they have to hunt through the cans of gooey garbage until they find their retainers because retainers cost a lot of money, and parents get mad if they get lost. Mr. Fridley always stands by the garbage cans to make sure kids who buy school lunches put their forks and spoons on a tray and not in the garbage. Whenever someone who wears a retainer scrapes his plate, Mr. Fridley says, "Look out. Don't lose your false teeth." This has cut down on lost retainers.

Mom says I take after Dad in one thing. My teeth are nice and straight which is a big saving right there.

Tuesday, January 9

Dear Mr. Pretend Henshaw,

My little cheesecake was missing at lunchtime which made me mad. I guess somebody noticed Joe Kelly's lunch was really mine. When I went to throw my lunchbag in the garbage, Mr. Fridley said, "Cheer up, Leigh, or you'll trip over your lower lip."

I said, "How would you feel if somebody was always stealing the good stuff from your lunch?"

He said, "What you need is a burglar alarm."

A burglar alarm on a lunchbag. I had to laugh at that, but I still wanted my cheesecake.

Dad should be phoning any day now. When I said that at supper (chili out of a can), Mom said for me not to get my hopes up, but I know Dad will remember this time. Mom never really says much about Dad, and when I ask why she divorced him, all she says is, "It takes two people to get a divorce." I guess she means the same way it takes two people to have a fight.

Tomorrow I am going to wrap my lunchbag in a lot of Scotch tape so nobody can sneak anything out of it.

Wednesday, January 10

Dear Mr. Pretend Henshaw,

It's funny how somebody says something,
and you can't forget it. I keep thinking about
Mr. Fridley saying I needed a burglar alarm on
my lunchbag. How could anybody put a burglar alarm on a paper bag? Today I used so
much Scotch tape on my lunchbag, I had a

hard time getting my lunch out. Everybody laughed.

Dad should phone today or tomorrow. Maybe if he came home he would know how I could make a burglar alarm for my lunchbag. He used to be good about helping me build things, except there wasn't much room in the mobile home we lived in, and you had to be careful where you pounded because a piece of plastic might break off something.

I read over the letter you wrote that time answering my questions and thought about your tips on how to write a book. One of the tips was *listen*. I guess you meant to listen and write down the way people talk, sort of like a play. This is what Mom and I said at supper (frozen chicken pies):

ME: Mom, how come you don't get married again?

MOM: Oh, I don't know. I guess men aren't that easy to find when you are out of school.

51

ME: But you go out sometimes. You went to dinner with Charlie a couple of times. What happened to him?

MOM: A couple of times was enough. That's the end of Charlie.

ME: How come?

MOM: (Thinks awhile.) Charlie is divorced and has three children to support. What he really wants is someone to help support Charlie.

ME: Oh. (Three sudden brothers or sisters was something to think about.) But I see men all around. There are lots of men.

MOM: But not the marrying kind. (Sort of laughs.) I guess I'm really afraid I might find another man who's in love with a truck.

ME: (I think about this and don't answer. Dad in love with a truck? What does she mean?)

MOM: Why are you asking all these questions all of a sudden?

ME: I was thinking if I had a father at home,

maybe he could show me how to make a burglar alarm for my lunchbag.

MOM: (Laughing.) There must be an easier way than my getting married again.

End of conversation

Dear Mr. Henshaw,

This is a real letter I am going to mail. Maybe I had better explain that I have written you many letters that are really my diary which I keep because you said so and because Mom still won't have the TV repaired. She wants my brain to stay in good shape. She says I will need my brain all my life.

Guess what? Today the school librarian stopped me in the hall and said she had something for me. She told me to come to the library. There she handed me your new book and said I could be the first to read it. I must have looked surprised. She said she knew how much I love your books since I check them out so often. Now I know Mr. Fridley isn't the only one who notices me.

I am on page 14 of *Beggar Bears.* It is a good book. I just wanted you to know that I am the first person around here to get to read it.

> Your No. 1 fan,
> Leigh Botts

Dear Mr. Henshaw,

I finished *Beggar Bears* in two nights. It is a really good book. At first I was surprised because it wasn't funny like your other books, but then I got to thinking (you said authors should think) and decided a book doesn't have to be funny to be good, although it often helps. This book did not need to be funny.

In the first chapter I thought it was going to be funny. I guess I expected it because of your other books and because the mother bear was teaching her twin cubs to beg from tourists in Yellowstone Park. Then when the mother died because a stupid tourist fed her a cupcake in a plastic bag and she ate the bag, too, I knew this was going to be a sad book. Winter was coming on, tourists were leaving the park and the little bears didn't know how to find food for themselves. When they hibernated and then woke up in the middle of winter because they had eaten all the wrong things and hadn't stored up enough fat, I almost cried. I sure was relieved when the nice ranger and his boy found the young bears and fed them and the next summer taught them to hunt for the right things to eat.

I wonder what happens to the fathers of bears. Do they just go away?

Sometimes I lie awake listening to the gas station pinging, and I worry because something might happen to Mom. She is so little compared to most moms, and she works so hard. I don't think Dad is that much interested in me. He didn't phone when he said he would.

I hope your book wins a million awards.

Sincerely,

Leigh Botts

Dear Mr. Henshaw,

Thank you for sending me the postcard with the picture of the lake and mountains and all that snow. Yes, I will continue to write in my diary even if I do have to pretend I am writing to you. You know something? I think I feel better when I write in my diary.

My teacher says my writing skills are improving. Maybe I really will be a famous author someday. She said our school along with some other schools is going to print (that means mimeograph) a book of work of young authors, and I should write a story for it. The writers of the best work will win a prize—lunch with a Famous Author and with winners from other schools. I hope the Famous Author is you.

I don't often get mail, but today I received two postcards, one from you and one from Dad in Kansas. His card showed a picture of a grain elevator. He said he would phone me sometime next week. I wish someday he would have to drive a load of something to Wyoming and would take me along so I could get to meet you.

That's all for now. I am going to try to think up a story. Don't worry. I won't send it to you to read. I know you are busy and I don't want to be a nuisance.

Your good friend,
Leigh Botts the First

FROM THE DIARY OF LEIGH BOTTS

Saturday, January 20

Dear Mr. Pretend Henshaw,

Every time I try to think up a story, it turns out to be like something someone else has written, usually you. I want to do what you said in your tips and write like *me*, not like somebody else. I'll keep trying because I want to be a Young Author with my story printed (mimeographed). Maybe I can't think of a story because I am waiting for Dad to call. I get so lonesome when I am alone at night when Mom is at her nursing class.

Yesterday somebody stole a piece of wedding cake from my lunchbag. It was the kind Catering by Katy packs in little white boxes for people to take home from weddings. Mr. Fridley noticed me scowling again and said, "So the lunchbag thief strikes again!"

I said, "Yeah, and my Dad didn't phone me."

He said, "Don't think you are the only boy around here with a father who forgets."

I wonder if this is true. Mr. Fridley keeps an eye on just about everything around school, so he probably knows.

I wish I had a grandfather like Mr. Fridley. He is so nice, sort of baggy and comfortable.

Monday, January 29

Dear Mr. Pretend Henshaw,

Dad still hasn't phoned, and he promised he would. Mom keeps telling me I shouldn't get my hopes up, because Dad sometimes forgets. I don't think he should forget what he wrote on a postcard. I feel terrible.

Tuesday, January 30

Dear Mr. Pretend Henshaw,

I looked in my book of highway maps and figured out that Dad should be back in Bakersfield by now, but he still hasn't phoned. Mom says I shouldn't be too hard on him, because a trucker's life isn't easy. Truckers sometimes lose some of their hearing in their left ear from the wind rushing past the driver's window. She says truckers get out of shape from sitting such long hours without exercise and from eating too much greasy food. Sometimes they get ulcers from the strain of trying to make good time on the highway. Time is money for a trucker. I think she is just trying to make me feel good, but I don't. I feel rotten.

I said, "If a trucker's life is so hard, how come Dad is in love with his truck?"

Mom said, "It's not really his truck he is in love with. He loves the feel of power when he is sitting high in his cab controlling a mighty machine. He loves the excitement of never knowing where his next trip will take him. He loves the mountains and the desert sunrises and the sight of orange trees heavy with oranges and the smell of fresh-mown alfalfa. I know, because I rode with him until you came along."

I still feel terrible. If Dad loves all those things so much, why can't he love me? And maybe if I hadn't been born, Mom might still be riding with Dad. Maybe I'm to blame for everything.

Wednesday, January 31

Dear Mr. Pretend Henshaw,

Dad still hasn't phoned. A promise is a promise, especially when it is in writing. When the phone does ring, it is always a call from one of the women Mom works with. I am filled with wrath (I got that out of a book, but not one of yours). I am mad at Mom for divorcing Dad. As she says, it takes two people to get a divorce, so I am mad at two people. I wish Bandit was here to keep me company. Bandit and I didn't get a divorce. They did.

Thursday, February 1

Dear Mr. Pretend Henshaw,

Today there was bad news in the paper. The sugar refinery is going to shut down. Even though Dad hauls cross-country now, I keep hoping sometime he might haul a really big load of sugar beets to Spreckels. Now maybe I'll never see him again.

Friday, February 2

Dear Mr. Pretend Henshaw,

I am writing this because I am trapped in my room with a couple of babies sleeping in baskets on my bed. Mom has some of her women friends over. They sit around drinking coffee or herb tea and talking about their problems which are mostly men, money, kids and landlords. Some of them piece quilts while they talk. They hope to sell them for extra money. It is better to stay in here with the babies than go out and say, "Hello, sure, I like school fine, yes, I guess I have grown," and all that.

Mom is right about Dad and his truck. I remember how exciting it was to ride with him and listen to calls on his Citizens' Band radio. Dad pointed out how hawks sit on telephone wires waiting for little animals to get run over so they won't have to bother to hunt. Dad says civilization is ruining hawks. He was hauling a gondola full of tomatoes that day, and he said that some tomatoes are grown specially so they are so strong they won't squash when loaded into a gondola. They may not taste like much, but they don't squash.

That day we had to stop at a weigh scale. Dad had used up enough diesel oil so his load was just under the legal weight, and the highway patrol didn't make him pay a fine for carrying too heavy a load. Then we had lunch at the truck stop. Everybody seemed to know Dad. The waitresses all said, "Well, look who just rolled in! Our old pal, Wild Bill," and things like that. Wild Bill from Bakersfield is the name Dad uses on his CB radio.

When Dad said, "Meet my kid," I stood up as tall as I could so they would think I was going to grow up as big as Dad. The waitresses all laughed a lot around Dad. For lunch we had chicken-fried steak, mashed potatoes with lots of gravy, peas out of a can, and apple pie with ice cream. Our waitress gave me extra ice cream to help me grow big like Dad. Most truckers ate real fast and left, but Dad kidded around awhile and played the video games. Dad always runs up a high score, no matter which machine he plays.

Mom's friends are collecting their babies, so I guess I can go to bed now.

Sunday, February 4

Dear Mr. Pretend Henshaw,

I hate my father.

Mom is usually home on Sunday, but this week there was a big golf tournament which means rich people have parties, so she had to go squirt deviled crab into about a million little cream puff shells. Mom never worries about meeting the rent when there is a big golf tournament.

I was all alone in the house, it was raining and I didn't have anything to read. I was supposed to scrub off some of the mildew on the bathroom walls with some smelly stuff, but I didn't because I was mad at Mom for divorcing Dad. I feel that way sometimes which makes me feel awful because I know how hard she has to work and try to go to school, too.

I kept looking at the telephone until I couldn't stand it any longer. I picked up the receiver and dialed Dad's number over in Bakersfield. I even remembered to dial 1 first because it was long distance. All I wanted was to hear the phone ringing in Dad's trailer which wouldn't cost Mom anything because nobody would answer.

Except Dad answered. I almost hung up. He wasn't off in some other state. He was in his trailer, and he hadn't phoned me. "You promised to phone me this week and you didn't," I said. I felt I had to talk to him.

"Take it easy, kid," he said. "I just didn't get around to it. I was going to call this evening. The week isn't over yet."

I thought about this.

"Something on your mind?" he asked.

I didn't know what to say, so I said, "My lunch. Somebody steals the good stuff out of my lunch."

"Find him and punch him in the nose," said Dad. I could tell he didn't think my lunch was important.

"I hoped you would call," I said. "I waited and waited." Then I was sorry I said it. I have some pride left.

"There was heavy snow in the mountains," he said. "I had to chain up on Highway 80 and lost time."

From my map book I know Highway 80 crosses the Sierra. I also know about putting chains on trucks. When the snow is heavy, truckers have to put chains on the drive wheels —all eight of them. Putting chains on eight big wheels in the snow is no fun. I felt a little better. "How's Bandit?" I asked, as long as we were talking.

There was a funny silence. For a minute I thought the line was dead. Then I knew something must have happened to my dog. "How's Bandit?" I asked again, louder in case Dad might have lost some of the hearing in his left ear from all that wind rushing by.

"Well, kid—" he began.

"My name is Leigh!" I almost yelled. "I'm not just some kid you met on the street."

"Keep your shirt on, Leigh," he said. "When I had to stop along with some other truckers to put on chains, I let Bandit out of the cab. I thought he would get right back in because it was snowing so hard, but after I chained up, he wasn't in the cab."

"Did you leave the door open for him?" I asked.

Big pause. "I could've sworn I did," he said which meant he didn't. Then he said, "I whistled and whistled, but Bandit didn't come. I couldn't wait any longer because the highway patrol was talking about closing Highway 80. I couldn't get stranded up there in the mountains when I had a deadline for delivering a load of TV sets to a dealer in Denver. I had to leave. I'm sorry, kid—Leigh—but that's the way it is."

"You left Bandit to freeze to death." I was crying from anger. How could he?

"Bandit knows how to take care of himself," said Dad. "I'll bet dollars to doughnuts he jumped into another truck that was leaving."

I wiped my nose on my sleeve. "Why would the driver let him?" I asked.

"Because he thought Bandit was lost," said Dad, "and he had to get on with his load before the highway was closed, the same as I did. He couldn't leave a dog to freeze."

"What about your CB radio?" I asked. "Didn't you send out a call?"

"Sure I did, but I didn't get an answer. Mountains cut down on reception," Dad told me.

I was about to say I understood, but here comes the bad part, the really bad part. I heard a boy's voice say, "Hey, Bill, Mom wants to know when we're going out to get the pizza?" I felt as if my insides were falling out. I hung up. I didn't want to hear any more, when Mom had to pay for the phone call. I didn't want to hear any more at all.

To be continued.

72

~~Dear Mr. Henshaw,~~

I don't have to pretend to write to Mr. Henshaw anymore. I have learned to say what I think on a piece of paper. And I don't hate my father either. I can't hate him. Maybe things would be easier if I could.

Yesterday after I hung up on Dad I flopped down on my bed and cried and swore and pounded my pillow. I felt so terrible about Bandit riding around with a strange trucker and Dad taking another boy out for pizza when I was all alone in the house with the mildewed bathroom when it was raining outside and I was hungry. The worst part of all was I knew if Dad took someone to a pizza place for dinner, he wouldn't have phoned me at all, no matter what he said. He would have too much fun playing video games.

Then I heard Mom's car stop out in front. I hurried and washed my face and tried to look as if I hadn't been crying, but I couldn't fool Mom. She came to the door of my room and said, "Hi, Leigh." I tried to look away, but she came closer in the dim light and said, "What's the matter, Leigh?"

"Nothing," I said, but she knew better. She sat down and put her arm around me.

I tried hard not to cry, but I couldn't help it. "Dad lost Bandit," I finally managed to say.

"Oh, Leigh," she said, and I blubbered out the whole story, pizza and all.

We just sat there awhile, and then I said, "Why did you have to go and marry him?"

"Because I was in love with him," she said.

"Why did you stop?" I asked.

"We just got married too young," she said. "Growing up in that little valley town with nothing but sagebrush, oil wells and jackrabbits there wasn't much to do. I remember at night how I used to look out at the lights of Bakersfield in the distance and wish I could live in a place like that, it looked so big and exciting. It seems funny now, but then it seemed like New York or Paris.

"After high school the boys mostly went to work in the oil fields or joined the army, and the girls got married. Some people went to college, but I couldn't get my parents interested in helping me. After graduation your Dad came along in a big truck and—well, that was that. He was big and handsome and nothing seemed to bother him, and the way he handled his rig—well, he seemed like a knight in shining armor. Things weren't too happy at home with your grandfather drinking and all, so your Dad and I ran off to Las Vegas and got married. I enjoyed riding with him until you came along, and—well, by that time I had had enough of highways and truck stops. I stayed home with you, and he was gone most of the time."

I felt a little better when Mom said she was tired of life on the road. Maybe I wasn't to blame after all. I remembered, too, how Mom and I were alone a lot and how I hated living in that mobile home. About the only places we ever went were the laundromat and the library. Mom read a lot and she used to read to me, too. She used to talk a lot about her elementary school principal, who was so excited about reading she had the whole school celebrate books and authors every April.

Now Mom went on. "I didn't think playing pinball machines in a tavern on Saturday night was fun anymore. Maybe I grew up and your father didn't."

Suddenly Mom began to cry. I felt terrible making Mom cry, so I began to cry some more, and we both cried until she said, "It's not your fault, Leigh. You mustn't ever think that. Your Dad has many good qualities. We just married too young, and he loves the excitement of life on the road, and I don't."

"But he lost Bandit," I said. "He didn't leave the cab door open for him when it was snowing."

"Maybe Bandit is just a bum," said Mom. "Some dogs are, you know. Remember how he jumped into your father's cab in the first place?

Maybe he was ready to move on to another truck."

She could be right, but I didn't like to think so. I was almost afraid to ask the next question, but I did. "Mom, do you still love Dad?"

"Please don't ask me," she said. I didn't know what to do, so I just sat there until she wiped her eyes and blew her nose and said, "Come on, Leigh, let's go out."

So we got in the car and drove to that fried chicken place and picked up a bucket of fried chicken. Then we drove down by the ocean and ate the chicken with rain sliding down the windshield and waves breaking on the rocks.

There were little cartons of mashed potatoes and gravy in the bucket of chicken, but someone had forgotten the plastic forks. We scooped up the potato with chicken bones, which made us laugh a little. Mom turned on the windshield wipers and out in the dark we could see the white of the breakers. We opened the windows so we could hear them roll in and break, one after another.

"You know," said Mom, "whenever I watch the waves, I always feel that no matter how bad things seem, life will still go on." That was how I felt, too, only I wouldn't have known how to say it, so I just said, "yeah." Then we drove home.

I feel a whole lot better about Mom. I'm not so sure about Dad even though, as she says, he has good qualities. I don't like to think that Bandit is a bum, but maybe Mom is right.

Today I felt so tired I didn't have to try to walk slow on the way to school. I just naturally did. Mr. Fridley had already raised the flags when I got there. The California bear was right side up so maybe Mr. Fridley didn't need me to help him after all. I just threw my lunch down on the floor and didn't care if anybody stole any of it. By lunchtime I was hungry again, and when I found my little cheesecake missing, I was mad all over again.

I'm going to get whoever steals from my lunch. Then he'll be sorry. I'll really fix him. Or maybe it's a her. Either way, I'll get even.

I tried to start a story for Young Writers. I got as far as the title which was *Ways to Catch a Lunchbag Thief*. A mousetrap in the bag was all I could think of, and anyway my title sounded too much like Mr. Henshaw's book.

Today during spelling I got so mad thinking about the lunchbag thief that I asked to be excused to go to the bathroom. As I went out into the hall, I scooped up the lunchbag closest to the door. I was about to drop-kick it down the hall when I felt a hand on my shoulder, and there was Mr. Fridley.

"What do you think you're doing?" he asked, and this time he wasn't being funny at all.

"Go ahead and tell the principal," I said. "See if I care."

"Maybe you don't," he said, "but I do."

That surprised me.

Then Mr. Fridley said, "I don't want to see a boy like you get into trouble, and that's where you're headed."

"I don't have any friends in this rotten school." I don't know why I said that. I guess I felt I had to say something.

"Who wants to be friends with someone who scowls all the time?" asked Mr. Fridley. "So you've got problems. Well, so has everyone else, if you take the trouble to notice."

I thought of Dad up in the mountains chaining up eight heavy wheels in the snow, and I thought of Mom squirting deviled crab into hundreds of little cream puff shells and making billions of tiny sandwiches for golfers to gulp and wondering if Catering by Katy would be able to pay her enough to make the rent.

"Turning into a mean-eyed lunch-kicker won't help anything," said Mr. Fridley. "You gotta think positively."

"How?" I asked.

"That's for you to figure out," he said and gave me a little shove toward my classroom.

Nobody noticed me put the lunchbag back on the floor.

Wednesday, February 7

Today after school I felt so rotten I decided to go for a walk. I wasn't going any special place, just walking. I had started down the street past the paint store and antique shops and bakery and all those places and on past the post office when I came to a sign that said BUTTER-

81

FLY TREES. I had heard a lot about those trees where monarch butterflies fly thousands of miles to spend the winter. I followed arrows until I came to a grove of mossy pine and eucalyptus trees with signs saying QUIET. There was a big sign that said WARNING. $500 FINE FOR MOLESTING BUTTERFLIES IN ANY WAY. I had to smile. Who would want to molest a butterfly?

The place was so quiet, almost like church, that I tiptoed. The grove was shady, and at first I thought all the signs about butterflies must be for some kind of ripoff for tourists, because I saw only three or four monarchs flitting around. Then I discovered some of the branches looked strange, as if they were covered with little brown sticks.

Then the sun came out from behind a cloud. The sticks began to move, and slowly they opened wings and turned into orange and black butterflies, thousands of them quivering on one tree. Then they began to float off through the trees in the sunshine. Those clouds

of butterflies were so beautiful I felt good all over and just stood there watching them until the fog began to roll in, and the butterflies came back and turned into brown sticks again. They made me think of a story Mom used to read me about Cinderella returning from the ball.

I felt so good I ran all the way home, and while I was running I had an idea for my story.

I also noticed that some of the shops had metal boxes that said "Alarm System" up near their roof. So does the gas station next door. I wonder what is in those boxes.

Thursday, February 8

Today when I came home from school, I leaned over the fence and yelled at a man who works in the gas station, "Hey, Chuck, what's in that box that says Alarm System on the side of the station?" I know his name is Chuck because it says so on his uniform.

"Batteries," Chuck told me. "Batteries and a bell."

Batteries are something to think about.

I started another story which I hope will get printed in the Young Writers' Yearbook. I think I will call it *The Ten-Foot Wax Man*. All the boys in my class are writing weird stories full of monsters, lasers and creatures from outer space. Girls seem to be writing mostly poems or stories about horses.

In the middle of working on my story I had a bright idea. If I took my lunch in a black lunchbox, the kind men carry, and got some batteries, maybe I really could rig up a burglar alarm.

Friday, February 9

Today I got a letter from Dad postmarked Albuquerque, New Mexico. At least I thought it was a letter, but when I tore it open, I found a twenty-dollar bill and a paper napkin. He had written on the napkin, "Sorry about Bandit. Here's $20. Go buy yourself an ice cream cone. Dad."

I was so mad I couldn't say anything. Mom read the napkin and said, "Your father doesn't mean you should actually buy an ice cream cone."

"Then why did he write it?" I asked.

"That's his way of trying to say he really is sorry about Bandit. He's just not very good at expressing feelings." Mom looked sad and said, "Some men aren't, you know."

"What am I supposed to do with the twenty dollars?" I asked, not that we couldn't use it.

"Keep it," said Mom. "It's yours, and it will come in handy."

When I asked if I had to write and thank

Dad, Mom gave me a funny look and said, "That's up to you."

Tonight I worked hard on my story for Young Writers about the ten-foot wax man and decided to save the twenty dollars toward a typewriter. When I get to be a real author I will need a typewriter.

Dear Mr. Henshaw,

I haven't written to you for a long time, because I know you are busy, but I need help with the story I am trying to write for the Young Writers' Yearbook. I got started, but I don't know how to finish it.

My story is about a man ten feet tall who drives a big truck, the kind my Dad drives. The man is made of wax, and every time he crosses the desert, he melts a little. He makes so many trips and melts so much he finally can't handle the gears or reach the brakes. That is as far as I can get. What should I do now?

The boys in my class who are writing about monsters just bring in a new monster on the last page to finish off the villains with a laser. That kind of ending doesn't seem right to me. I don't know why.

Please help. Just a postcard will do.

> Hopefully,
> Leigh Botts

P.S. Until I started trying to write a story, I wrote in my diary almost every day.

Dear Mr. Henshaw,

Thank you for answering my letter. I was surprised that you had trouble writing stories when you were my age. I think you are right. Maybe I am not ready to write a story. I understand what you mean. A character in a story should solve a problem or change in some way. I can see that a wax man who melts until he's a puddle wouldn't be there to solve anything and melting isn't the sort of change you mean. I suppose somebody could turn up on the last page and make candles out of him. That would change him all right, but that is not the ending I want.

I asked Miss Martinez if I had to write a story for Young Writers, and she said I could write a poem or a description.

Your grateful friend,
Leigh

P.S. I bought a copy of *Ways to Amuse a Dog* at a garage sale. I hope you don't mind.

FROM THE DIARY OF LEIGH BOTTS
VOL. 2

Thursday, March 1

I am getting behind in this diary for several reasons, including working on my story and writing to Mr. Henshaw (really, not just pretend). I also had to buy a new notebook because I had filled up the first one.

The same day, I bought a beat-up black lunchbox in the thrift shop down the street and started carrying my lunch in it. The kids were surprised, but nobody made fun of me, because a black lunchbox isn't the same as one of those square boxes covered with cartoon characters that first and second graders carry. A couple of boys asked if it was my Dad's. I just grinned and said, "Where do you think I got it?" The next day my little slices of salami rolled around cream cheese were gone, but I expected that. But I'll get that thief yet. I'll make him really sorry he ate all the best things out of my lunch.

Next I went to the library for books on batteries. I took out a couple of easy books on electricity, really easy, because I have never given much thought to batteries. About all I know is that when you want to use a flashlight, the battery is usually dead.

I finally gave up on my story about the ten-foot wax man, which was really pretty dumb. I thought I would write a poem about butterflies for Young Writers because a poem can be short, but it is hard to think about butterflies and burglar alarms at the same time, so I studied electricity books instead. The books didn't have directions for an alarm in a lunchbox, but I learned enough about batteries and switches and insulated wires, so I think I can figure it out myself.

Back to the poem tonight. The only rhyme I can think of for "butterfly" is "flutter by." I can think up rhymes like "trees" and "breeze" which are pretty boring, and then I think of "wheeze" and "sneeze." A poem about butterflies wheezing and sneezing seems silly, and anyway a couple of girls are already writing poems about monarch butterflies that flutter by.

Sometimes I start a letter to Dad thanking him for the twenty dollars, but I can't finish that either. I don't know why.

Today I took my lunchbox and Dad's twenty dollars to the hardware store and looked around. I found an ordinary light switch, a little battery and a cheap doorbell. While I was looking around for the right kind of insulated wire, a man who had been watching me (boys my age always get watched when they go into stores) asked if he could help me. He was a nice old gentleman who said, "What are you planning to make, son?" *Son.* He called me son, and my Dad calls me kid. I didn't want to tell the man, but when he looked at the things I was holding, he grinned and said, "Having trouble with your lunch, aren't you?" I nodded and said, "I'm trying to make a burglar alarm."

He said, "That's what I guessed. I've had workmen in here with the same problem."

It turned out that I needed a 6-volt lantern battery instead of the battery I had picked out. He gave me a couple of tips and, after I paid for the things, a little slap on the back and said, "Good luck, son."

I tore home with all the things I bought. First I made a sign for my door that said

KEEP OUT
MOM
THAT MEANS YOU

Then I went to work fastening one wire from the battery to the switch and from the other side of the switch to the doorbell. Then I fastened a second wire from the battery to the doorbell. It took me a while to get it right. Then I taped the battery in one corner of the lunchbox and the doorbell in another. I stood the switch up at the back of the box and taped that in place, too.

Here I ran into a problem. I thought I could take the wire clamp meant to hold a thermos bottle inside the lunchbox lid and hook it under the switch if I reached in carefully as I closed the box. The clamp wasn't quite long enough. After some thinking and experimenting, I twisted a wire loop onto it. Then I closed the

box just enough so I could get my hand inside and push the wire loop over the button on the switch before I took my hand out and closed the box.

Then I opened the box. My burglar alarm worked! That bell inside the box went off with a terrible racket that brought Mom to my door. "Leigh, what on earth is going on in there?" she shouted above the alarm.

I let her in and gave her a demonstration of my burglar alarm. She laughed and said it was a great invention. One thing was bothering me. Would my sandwich muffle the bell? Mom must have been wondering the same thing, because she suggested taping a piece of cardboard into the lid that would make a shelf for my sandwich. I did, and that worked, too.

I can't wait until Monday.

Monday, March 5
Today Mom packed my lunch carefully, and we tried the alarm to see if it still worked. It did,

good and loud. When I got to school, Mr. Fridley said, "Nice to see you smiling, Leigh. You should try it more often."

I parked my lunchbox behind the partition and waited. I waited all morning for the alarm to go off. Miss Martinez asked if I had my mind on my work. I pretended I did, but all the time I was really waiting for my alarm to go off so I could dash back behind the partition and tackle the thief. When nothing happened, I began to worry. Maybe the loop had somehow slipped off the switch on the way to school.

Lunchtime came. The alarm still hadn't gone off. We all picked up our lunches and went off to the cafeteria. When I set my box on the table in front of me, I realized I had a problem, a big problem. If the loop hadn't slipped off the switch, my alarm was still triggered. I just sat there, staring at my lunchbox, not knowing what to do.

"How come you're not eating?" Barry asked with his mouth full. Barry's sandwiches are never cut in half, and he always takes a big bite out of one side to start.

Everybody at the table was looking at me. I thought about saying I wasn't hungry, but I was. I thought about taking my lunchbox out into the hall to open, but if the alarm was still triggered, there was no way I could open it quietly. Finally I thought, Here goes. I unsnapped the two fasteners on the box and held my breath as I opened the lid.

Wow! My alarm went off! The noise was so loud it startled everybody at the table including me and made everyone in the cafeteria look around. I looked up and saw Mr. Fridley grinning at me over by the garbage can. Then I turned off the alarm.

Suddenly everybody seemed to be noticing me. The principal, who always prowls around keeping an eye on things at lunchtime, came over to examine my lunchbox. He said, "That's quite an invention you have there."

"Thanks," I said, pleased that the principal seemed to like my alarm.

Some of the teachers came out of their lunchroom to see what the noise was all about. I had to give a demonstration. It seems I wasn't the only one who had things stolen from my lunch, and all the kids said they wanted lunchboxes with alarms, too, even those whose lunches were never good enough to have anything stolen. Barry said he would like an alarm like that on the door of his room at home. I began to feel

101

like some sort of hero. Maybe I'm not so medium after all.

One thing bothers me, though. I still don't know who's been robbing my lunch.

Tuesday, March 6

Today Barry asked me to come home with him to see if I could help him rig up a burglar alarm for his room because he has a bunch of little sisters and stepsisters who get into his stuff. I thought I could, because I had seen an alarm like that in one of the electricity books from the library.

Barry lives in a big old house that is sort of cheerful and messy, with little girls all over the place. As it turned out, Barry didn't have the right kind of battery so we just fooled around looking at his models. Barry never uses directions when he puts models together, because the directions are too hard and spoil the fun. He throws them away and figures out how the pieces fit by himself.

I still don't know what to write for Young

Writers, but I was feeling so good I finally wrote to Dad to thank him for the twenty dollars because I had found a good use for it even if I couldn't save it all toward a typewriter. I didn't say much.

I wonder if Dad will marry the pizza boy and his mother. I worry about that a lot.

Thursday, March 15

This week several kids turned up with lunchboxes with burglar alarms. You know that song about the hills ringing with the sound of music? Well, you might say our cafeteria rang with the sound of burglar alarms. The fad didn't last very long, and after a while I didn't even bother to set my alarm. Nobody has robbed my lunchbox since I set it off that day.

I never did find out who the thief was, and now that I stop to think about it, I am glad. If he had set off the alarm when my lunchbox was in the classroom, he would have been in trouble, big trouble. Maybe he was just somebody whose mother packed bad lunches—jelly sand-

103

wiches on that white bread that tastes like Kleenex. Or maybe he had to pack his own lunches and there was never anything good in the house to put in them. I have seen people look into their lunches, take out the cookies and throw the rest in the garbage. Mr. Fridley always looks worried when they do this.

I'm not saying robbing lunchboxes is right. I am saying I'm glad I don't know who the thief was, because I have to go to school with him.

Friday, March 16

Tonight I was staring at a piece of paper trying to think of something to write for Young Writers when the phone rang. Mom told me to answer because she was washing her hair.

It was Dad. My stomach felt as if it was dropping to the floor, the way it always does when I hear his voice. "How're you doing, kid?" he asked.

"Fine," I said, thinking of the success of my burglar alarm. "Great."

"I got your letter," he said.

"That's good," I said. His call took me so by surprise that I could feel my heart pounding, and I couldn't think of anything to say until I asked, "Have you found another dog to take Bandit's place?" I think what I really meant was, Have you found another boy to take my place?

"No, but I ask about him on my CB," Dad told me. "He may turn up yet."

"I hope so." This conversation was going no place. I really didn't know what to say to my father. It was embarrassing.

Then Dad surprised me. He asked, "Do you ever miss your old Dad?"

I had to think a minute. I missed him all right, but I couldn't seem to get the words out. My silence must have bothered him because he asked, "Are you still there?"

"Sure, Dad, I miss you," I told him. It was

true, but not as true as it had been a couple of months ago. I still wanted him to pull up in front of the house in his big rig, but now I knew I couldn't count on it.

"Sorry I don't get over your way more often," he said. "I hear the sugar refinery in Spreckels is closing down."

"I read about it in the paper," I said.

"Is your mother handy?" he asked.

"I'll see," I said even though by then she was standing by the phone with her hair wrapped in a towel. She shook her head. She didn't want to talk to Dad.

"She's washing her hair," I said.

"Tell her I'll manage to send your support check sometime next week," he said. "So long, kid. Keep your nose clean."

"So long, Dad," I answered. "Drive carefully." I guess he'll never learn that my name is Leigh and that my nose is clean. Maybe he thinks I'll never learn that he drives carefully. He doesn't really. He's a good driver, but he speeds to make time whenever he can avoid the highway patrol. All truckers do.

After that I couldn't get back to thinking about Young Writers, so I picked up *Ways to Amuse a Dog* and read it for the thousandth time. I read harder books now, but I still feel good when I read that book. I wonder where Mr. Henshaw is.

Saturday, March 17

Today is Saturday, so this morning I walked to the butterfly trees again. The grove was quiet and peaceful, and because the sun was shining, I stood there a long time, looking at the orange butterflies floating through the gray and green leaves and listening to the sound of the ocean on the rocks. There aren't as many butterflies now. Maybe they are starting to go north for the summer. I thought I might write about them in prose instead of poetry, but on the way home I got to thinking about Dad and one time when he took me along when he was

107

hauling grapes to a winery and what a great day it had been.

Tuesday, March 20

Yesterday Miss Neely, the librarian, asked if I had written anything for the Young Writers' Yearbook, because all writing had to be turned in by tomorrow. When I told her I hadn't, she said I still had twenty-four hours and why didn't I get busy? So I did, because I really would like to meet a Famous Author. My story about the ten-foot wax man went into the wastebasket. Next I tried to start a story called *The Great Lunchbox Mystery*, but I couldn't seem to turn my lunchbox experience into a story because I don't know who the thief (thieves) was (were), and I don't want to know.

Finally I dashed off a description of the time I rode with my father when he was trucking the load of grapes down Highway 152 through Pacheco Pass to a winery. I put in things like the signs that said STEEP GRADE, TRUCKS USE LOW GEAR and how Dad down-shifted and how skillful he was handling a long, heavy load on the curves. I put in about the hawks on the telephone wires and about that high peak where Black Bart's lookout used to watch for travelers coming through the pass so he could signal to Black Bart to rob them, and how the leaves on the trees along the stream at the bottom of the pass were turning yellow and how good tons of grapes smelled in the sun. I left out the part about the waitresses and the video games. Then I copied the whole thing over in case neatness counts and gave it to Miss Neely.

Saturday, March 24

Mom said I had to invite Barry over to our house for supper because I have been going to his house after school so often. We had been working on a burglar alarm for his room which we finally got to work with some help from a library book.

I wasn't sure Barry would like to come to our house which is so small compared to his, but he accepted when I invited him.

Mom cooked a casserole full of good things like ground beef, chilies, tortillas, tomatoes and cheese. Barry said he really liked eating at our house because he got tired of eating with a bunch of little sisters waving spoons and drumsticks. That made me happy. It helps to have a friend.

Barry says his burglar alarm still works. The trouble is, his little sisters think it's fun to open his door to set it off. Then they giggle and hide.

This was driving his mother crazy, so he finally had to disconnect it. We all laughed about this. Barry and I felt good about making something that worked even if he can't use it.

Barry saw the sign on my door that said KEEP OUT MOM THAT MEANS YOU. He asked if my Mom really stays out of my room. I said, "Sure, if I keep things picked up." Mom is not a snoop.

Barry said he wished he could have a room nobody ever went into. I was glad Barry didn't ask to use the bathroom. Maybe I'll start scrubbing off the mildew after all.

Sunday, March 25

I keep thinking about Dad and how lonely he sounded and wondering what happened to the pizza boy. I don't like to think about Dad being lonesome, but I don't like to think about the pizza boy cheering him up either.

Tonight at supper (beans and franks) I got up my courage to ask Mom if she thought Dad

111

would get married again. She thought awhile and then said, "I don't see how he could afford to. He has big payments to make on the truck, and the price of diesel oil goes up all the time, and when people can't afford to build houses or buy cars, he won't be hauling lumber or cars."

I thought this over. I know that a license for a truck like his costs over a thousand dollars a year. "But he always sends my support payments," I said, "even if he is late sometimes."

"Yes, he does that," agreed my mother. "Your father isn't a bad man by any means."

Suddenly I was mad and disgusted with the whole thing. "Then why don't you two get married again?" I guess I wasn't very nice about the way I said it.

Mom looked me straight in the eye. "Because your father will never grow up," she said. I knew that was all she would ever say about it.

Tomorrow they give out the Young Writers' Yearbook! Maybe I will be lucky and get to go have lunch with the Famous Author.

Monday, March 26

Today wasn't the greatest day of my life. When our class went to the library, I saw a stack of Yearbooks and could hardly wait for Miss Neely to hand them out. When I finally got mine and opened it to the first page, there was a monster story, and I saw I hadn't won first prize. I kept turning. I didn't win second prize which went to a poem, and I didn't win third or fourth prize, either. Then I turned another page and saw Honorable Mention and under it:

A DAY ON DAD'S RIG
by
LEIGH M. BOTTS

There was my title with my name under it in print, even if it was mimeographed print. I can't say I wasn't disappointed because I hadn't won a prize, I was. I was really disappointed about not getting to meet the mysterious Famous Author, but I liked seeing my name in print.

Some kids were mad because they didn't win or even get something printed. They said they wouldn't ever try to write again which I think is pretty dumb. I have heard that real authors sometimes have their books turned down. I figure you win some, you lose some.

Then Miss Neely announced that the Famous Author the winners would get to have lunch with was Angela Badger. The girls were more excited than the boys because Angela Badger writes mostly about girls with problems like big feet or pimples or something. I would still like to meet her because she is, as they say, a real live author, and I've never met a real live author. I am glad Mr. Henshaw isn't the author because then I would *really* be disappointed that I didn't get to meet him.

Friday, March 30

Today turned out to be exciting. In the middle of second period Miss Neely called me out of class and asked if I would like to go have lunch with Angela Badger. I said, "Sure, how come?"

Miss Neely explained that the teachers discovered that the winning poem had been copied out of a book and wasn't original so the girl who submitted it would not be allowed to go and would I like to go in her place? Would I!

Miss Neely telephoned Mom at work for permission and I gave my lunch to Barry because my lunches are better than his. The other winners were all dressed up, but I didn't care. I have noticed that authors like Mr. Henshaw usually wear old plaid shirts in the pictures on the back of their books. My shirt is just as old as his, so I knew it was OK.

Miss Neely drove us in her own car to the Holiday Inn, where some other librarians and their winners were waiting in the lobby. Then Angela Badger arrived with Mr. Badger, and we were all led into the dining room which was pretty crowded. One of the librarians who was a sort of Super Librarian told the winners to sit at a long table with a sign that said Reserved. Angela Badger sat in the middle and some of the girls pushed to sit beside her. I sat across from her. Super Librarian explained that we could choose our lunch from the salad bar. Then all the librarians went off and sat at a table with Mr. Badger.

There I was face to face with a real live author who seemed like a nice lady, plump with wild hair, and I couldn't think of a thing to say because I hadn't read her books. Some girls told her how much they loved her books, but some of the boys and girls were too shy to say anything. Nothing seemed to happen until Mrs. Badger said, "Why don't we all go help ourselves to lunch at the salad bar?"

What a mess! Some people didn't understand about salad bars, but Mrs. Badger led the way and we helped ourselves to lettuce and bean salad and potato salad and all the usual stuff they lay out on salad bars. A few of the younger kids were too short to reach anything but the bowls on the first rows. They weren't doing too well until Mrs. Badger helped them out. Getting lunch took a long time, longer than in a school cafeteria, and when we carried our plates back to our table, people at other tables ducked and dodged as if they expected us to dump our lunches on their heads. All one boy had on his plate was a piece of lettuce and a slice of tomato because he thought he was going to get to go back for roast beef and fried chicken. We had to straighten him out and explain that all we got was salad. He turned red and went back for more salad.

I was still trying to think of something interesting to say to Mrs. Badger while I chased garbanzo beans around my plate with a fork. A couple of girls did all the talking, telling Mrs. Badger how they wanted to write books exactly like hers. The other librarians were busy talking and laughing with Mr. Badger who seemed to be a lot of fun.

Mrs. Badger tried to get some of the shy people to say something without much luck, and I still couldn't think of anything to say to a lady who wrote books about girls with big feet or pimples. Finally Mrs. Badger looked straight at me and asked, "What did you write for the Yearbook?"

I felt myself turn red and answered, "Just something about a ride on a truck."

"Oh!" said Mrs. Badger. "So you're the author of *A Day on Dad's Rig!*"

Everyone was quiet. None of us had known the real live author would have read what we

had written, but she had and she remembered my title.

"I just got honorable mention," I said, but I was thinking, She called me an author. *A real live author called me an author.*

"What difference does that make?" asked Mrs. Badger. "Judges never agree. I happened to like *A Day on Dad's Rig* because it was written by a boy who wrote honestly about something he knew and had strong feelings about. You made me feel what it was like to ride down a steep grade with tons of grapes behind me."

"But I couldn't make it into a story," I said, feeling a whole lot braver.

"Who cares?" said Mrs. Badger with a wave of her hand. She's the kind of person who wears rings on her forefingers. "What do you expect? The ability to write stories comes later, when you have lived longer and have more understanding. *A Day on Dad's Rig* was splendid work for a boy your age. You wrote like *you*, and you did not try to imitate someone

119

else. This is one mark of a good writer. Keep it up."

I noticed a couple of girls who had been saying they wanted to write books exactly like Angela Badger exchange embarrassed looks.

"Gee, thanks," was all I could say. The waitress began to plunk down dishes of ice cream. Everyone got over being shy and began to ask Mrs. Badger if she wrote in pencil or on the typewriter and did she ever have books rejected and were her characters real people and did she ever have pimples when she was a girl like the girl in her book and what did it feel like to be a famous author?

I didn't think answers to those questions were very important, but I did have one question I wanted to ask which I finally managed to get in at the last minute when Mrs. Badger was autographing some books people had brought.

"Mrs. Badger," I said, "did you ever meet Boyd Henshaw?"

"Why, yes," she said, scribbling away in someone's book. "I once met him at a meeting of librarians where we were on the same program."

"What's he like?" I asked over the head of a girl crowding up with her book.

"He's a very nice young man with a wicked twinkle in his eye," she answered. I think I have known that since the time he answered my questions when Miss Martinez made us write to an author.

On the ride home everybody was chattering about Mrs. Badger this, and Mrs. Badger that. I didn't want to talk. I just wanted to think. A real live author had called *me* an author. A real live author had told me to keep it up. Mom was proud of me when I told her.

The gas station stopped pinging a long time ago, but I wanted to write all this down while I remembered. I'm glad tomorrow is Saturday. If I had to go to school I would yawn. I wish Dad was here so I could tell him all about today.

Dear Mr. Henshaw,

I'll keep this short to save you time reading it. I had to tell you something. You were right. I wasn't ready to write an imaginary story. But guess what! I wrote a true story which won Honorable Mention in the Yearbook. Maybe next year I'll write something that will win first or second place. Maybe by then I will be able to write an imaginary story.

I just thought you would like to know. Thank you for your help. If it hadn't been for you, I might have handed in that dumb story about the melting wax trucker.

Your friend, the author,
Leigh Botts

P.S. I still write in the diary you started me on.

FROM THE DIARY OF LEIGH BOTTS

Saturday, March 31

This morning the sun was shining, so Barry and I mailed my letter to Mr. Henshaw and then walked over to see if there were still any butterflies in the grove. We only saw three or four, so I guess most of them have gone north for the summer. Then we walked down to the little park at Lovers Point and sat on a rock watching sailboats on the bay for a while. When clouds began to blow in we walked back to my house.

A tractor without a trailer attached was parked in front. Dad's! I began to run, and Dad and Bandit got out of the cab.

"So long, I gotta go," yelled Barry who has

heard a lot about Dad and Bandit and who
understands about parents and divorce.

Dad and I just stood there looking at one
another until I said, "Hi, Dad. Seen any shoes
on the highway lately?"

"Lots of them." Dad grinned half a grin, not

126

like his old self. "Boots, sneakers, all kinds."

Bandit came over to me, wagging his tail and looking happy. He was wearing a new red bandanna around his neck.

"How're you doing, kid?" asked Dad. "I brought your dog back."

"Gee, thanks," I said, hugging Bandit. Dad's stomach hung over his belt, and he wasn't as tall as I remembered him.

"You've grown," he said which is what grownups always say when they don't know what else to say to kids.

Did Dad expect me to stop growing just because he hadn't been around? "How did you find Bandit?" I asked.

"By asking every day over my CB," he said. "I finally got an answer from a trucker who said he had picked up a lost dog in a snowstorm in the Sierra, a dog that was still riding with him. Last week we turned up in the same line at a weigh scale."

"I'm sure glad you got him back," I said, and after trying to think of something else to say, I asked, "How come you're not hauling anything?" I think I hoped he would say he had driven all the way from Bakersfield just to bring Bandit back to me.

"I'm waiting for a reefer to be loaded with broccoli in Salinas," he told me. "Since it wasn't far, I thought I'd take a run over here before I take off for Ohio."

So Dad had come to see me just because of broccoli. After all these months when I had longed to see him, it took a load of broccoli to get him here. I felt let down and my feelings hurt. They hurt so much I couldn't think of anything to say.

Just then Mom drove up and got out of her old car which looked little and shabby beside Dad's big rig.

"Hello, Bill," she said.

"Hello, Bonnie," he said.

We all just stood there with Bandit waving his tail, until Dad said, "Aren't you going to ask me in?"

"Sure, come on in," said Mom. Bandit followed us down the walk past the duplex to our little house and came inside with us. "How about a cup of coffee?" Mom asked Dad.

"Sure," agreed Dad, looking around. "So this is where you two live." Then he sat down on the couch.

"This is where we live as long as we can pay the rent," said Mom in a flat voice. "And it can never be towed away." Mom really hated that mobile home we used to live in.

Dad looked tired and sad in a way I had never seen him look before. While Mom fussed around making coffee, I showed him the burglar alarm I had made for my lunchbox. He worked it a couple of times and said, "I always knew I had a smart kid."

Mom was taking such a long time making coffee I felt I had to entertain Dad so I showed him my Yearbook and what I had written. He read it and said, "Funny, but I still think about that day every time I haul grapes to a winery. I'm glad you remember it, too." That made me feel good. He looked at me awhile as if he expected to see . . . I don't know what. Then he rumpled my hair and said, "You're smarter than your old man."

That embarrassed me. I didn't know how to answer.

Finally Mom brought in two mugs of coffee. She gave one to Dad and carried hers over to a chair. They just sat there looking at one another over the rims of their mugs. I wanted to yell, Do something! Say something! Don't just sit there!

Finally Dad said, "I miss you, Bonnie."

I had a feeling I didn't want to hear this conversation, but I didn't know how to get out of there so I got down on the floor and hugged Bandit who rolled over on his back to have his stomach scratched just as if he had never been away.

"I'm sorry," said Mom. I think she meant she was sorry Dad missed her. Or maybe she was sorry about everything. I don't know.

"Have you found someone else?" asked Dad.

"No," said Mom.

"I think about you a lot on the long hauls," said Dad, "especially at night."

"I haven't forgotten you," said Mom.

"Bonnie, is there any chance—" Dad began.

"No," said Mom in a sad, soft voice. "There isn't a chance."

"Why not?" asked Dad.

"Too many lonely days and nights not knowing where you were, too much waiting for phone calls you forgot to make because you were whooping it up at some truck stop," said Mom. "Too many boring Saturday nights in some noisy tavern. Too many broken promises. Things like that."

"Well . . ." said Dad and set his mug down. "That's what I came to find out, so I might as well be going." He hadn't even finished his coffee. He stood up and so did I. Then he gave me a big hug, and for a minute I wanted to hang on to him and never let him go.

"So long, son," he said. "I'll try to get over to see you more often."

"Sure, Dad," I said. I had learned by now that I couldn't count on anything he said.

Mom came to the door. Suddenly Dad hugged her, and to my surprise, she hugged

132

him back. Then he turned and ran down the steps. When he reached his rig, he called back, "Take good care of Bandit."

I thought of Dad hauling a forty-foot refrigerated trailer full of broccoli over the Sierra and the Rockies and across the plains and all those places in my book of road maps until he got to Ohio. Personally I would be happy to see all the broccoli in California trucked to Ohio because it's not my favorite vegetable, but I didn't like to think of Dad alone on that long haul driving all day and most of the night, except when he snatched a few hours' sleep in his bunk, and thinking of Mom.

"Dad, wait!" I yelled and ran out to him. "Dad, you keep Bandit. You need him more than I do." Dad hesitated until I said, "Please take him. I don't have any way to amuse him."

Dad smiled at that, and whistled, and Bandit jumped into the cab as if that was what he really wanted to do all along.

"So long, Leigh," Dad said and started the motor. Then he leaned out and said, "You're a good kid, Leigh. I'm proud of you, and I'll try not to let you down." Then as he drove off, he yelled, "See you around!" and sounded more the way I had remembered him.

When I went inside, Mom was sipping her coffee and sort of staring into space. I went into my room, shut the door and sat listening to the gas station go ping-ping, ping-ping. Maybe it was broccoli that brought Dad to Salinas, but he had come the rest of the way because he really wanted to see us. He had really missed us. I felt sad and a whole lot better at the same time.